MITCHOO
A Very Special Bear

S Hardingham

ISBN 1 84401 523 8

First Published 2005 by
ATHENA PRESS
Queen's House, 2 Holly Road
Twickenham, TW1 4EG
United Kingdom

Printed for Athena Press

MITCHOO
A Very Special Bear

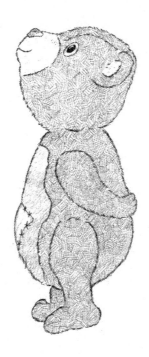

S Hardingham

One day, Chelsea,
Paige and Amy

were helping their mum
clear out the garage.

The girls discovered all sorts of things, including a tatty old teddy bear.

'Mum, whose is this?' asked Chelsea, picking up the teddy bear.

'That,' replied Mum, 'is a very special teddy bear made for me by my grandmother when I was a little girl.'

'What's special about him? He stinks!' said Paige, wrinkling her nose up.

Mum laughed. 'Aahh,' she replied, 'you girls look after him and I promise he'll look after you.'

'What's his name?' asked Amy.

'Mitchoo,' said Mum.

'*Mitchoo?* What kind of name is that?' exclaimed Chelsea.

'A special name for a special bear,'
replied Mum, with a knowing smile.

The girls were in the playroom.
'I'm bored,' said Chelsea.

'So am I,' said Paige.

'And me!' added Amy.

'Well, we can't go out, it's raining,'
sighed Chelsea.

Suddenly she had an idea. 'I know, we could bath Mitchoo. You were right, Paige, he does stink!'

Paige and Amy grinned. They loved nothing more than to play with water. Bathing Mitchoo was a great idea!

Mitchoo, however, didn't agree. As Amy was about to grab him he pulled away. Amy stood back in surprise.

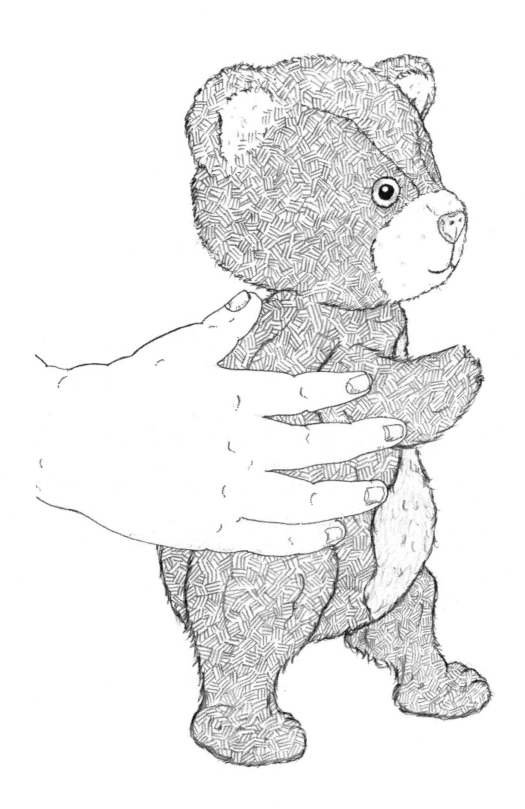

'What's wrong?' asked Paige.

'Mitchoo moved,' Amy replied quietly.

'Don't be silly,' laughed Chelsea.
'He's a teddy bear, and they don't move
by themselves.'

'No?' said a cross voice. 'Well I do.'

The girls froze. It seemed like for ever before anyone moved.

Finally Chelsea went up to the bear.

'Erm, are you magic?' she asked in a whisper.

'Yes, and to keep my magic I mustn't get wet, so no baths!'

'OK,' said Chelsea slowly. 'Would you like to play with us instead?'

'Of course,' replied the bear. 'Isn't that what I'm here for?'

'What shall we play?' asked Chelsea.

'I know,' said Mitchoo, 'let's play hide and seek. Amy, you look for us after counting to ten.'

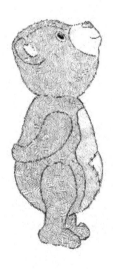

'How do you know my name?' asked Amy, surprised.

'Because he's magic!' answered Chelsea and Paige together.

Amy stood facing the wall as she counted to ten. '…Eight, nine, ten. Ready or not, here I come!' she called.

Almost immediately Amy noticed the curtain moving. She smiled as she pulled it back to find Paige. Feeling rather proud of herself, Amy went on to look for the other two.

It wasn't long before she found
Chelsea hiding under the bed.
Now there was only Mitchoo to find.

'Mitchoo, I'm coming to get you!' she chanted happily.

'Oh no you're not!' said Mitchoo.

The voice seemed to be right behind Amy, so much so that she jumped when she heard it. She turned around and smiled when she noticed the wardrobe door was slightly open.

She crept up to it and then quickly pulled it open, expecting Mitchoo to be hiding in there, but the wardrobe was empty.

All of a sudden the girls heard
Mitchoo laugh.

'Mitchooooo, where are you?'
called Amy.

Amy looked at her sisters for a clue.

'No point looking at us,' said Chelsea.
'We thought he was in the wardrobe too.'

Mitchoo laughed again.
'Do you give up?' he called.

'Yes,' replied Amy.
She was getting fed up now.

'Here I am!' said Mitchoo, and he
seemed to appear out of nowhere.

The girls stared at him as it dawned on them that Mitchoo really *was* magical! Chelsea, Paige and Amy knew that as long as they had Mitchoo there were a lot more fun and games to come.

'I love you!' shrieked Amy as she hugged Mitchoo.
'You are the best bear ever!'

The End

CPSIA information can be obtained
at www.ICGtesting.com
Printed in the USA
LVOW03s1741011215

464812LV00025BA/358/P